Heartbeats of Imagined Lives:

A Tribute in Poetry
to Fictional Favorites

Brandon Michaels

Heartbeats of Imagined Lives:

A Tribute in Poetry to Fictional Favorites

X

@AuthorBMichaels

www.authorbrandonmichaels.com

This book is protected under the copyright laws of the United States of America. Any reproduction or other unauthorized use of the material or artwork herein is prohibited without the author's or publisher's express written permission.

Dedication

To those who dream among the stars, who journey through pages, screens, and beyond—your passion for stories makes every heartbeat worthwhile.

3/27/2025

Dear Readers,

In creating "Heartbeats of Imagined Lives," I embarked on a deeply personal journey to honor the characters and stories that have profoundly moved me. These poems arose from moments when fictional lives felt incredibly real—moments that stirred my imagination, pulled at my heartstrings, and ignited a spark of inspiration within me. Each poem is my way of expressing gratitude and affection for the heroes and dreamers who have influenced my life.

I hope this collection resonates with you, reminding you of your own beloved characters and the power stories hold to transform, comfort, and inspire. May these verses connect us in our shared love for the extraordinary worlds we cherish.

Sincerely,

Brandon Michaels

Table of Contents

Stephen King

Andy Dufresne

Behind gray walls and iron bars,
Where hope lies buried, counting scars,
A quiet man with patient eyes,
Andy dreams beneath dark skies.

Accused of crime he did not do,
He faced a judgment harsh, untrue.
In Shawshank's gloom, alone confined,
Yet freedom lived within his mind.

With gentle voice and humble grace,
He carved his life in that hard place.
A library built from broken dreams,
A whisper soft, where sunlight beams.

He tunneled slow through years unseen,
With pockets full of dust and dreams.
And while the guards slept unaware,
Andy planned escape with care.

The thunder crashed, the lightning flashed,
Through filth and rain, to freedom dashed.
Cleansed by storms, he reached the shore,
Where chains of Shawshank bound no more.

Now waves caress the distant sand,
With open skies, a new life's planned.
A friend awaits beneath the sun,
For Andy's hope, at last, has won.

Red's Redemption

In Shawshank walls, I learned to cope,
A prisoner bound, devoid of hope.
They called me Red, the man who knew,
Who got you things, whose word held true.

My sentence long, my spirit worn,
In iron bars, my dreams were torn.
The years rolled by in endless flow,
A life of gray, imprisoned slow.

Then Andy came, quiet, serene—
His eyes held truths I'd never seen.
With subtle strength, and steady heart,
He showed me hope—a brand-new start.

When darkness fell, he slipped away,
Escaped the chains, embraced the day.
He taught my soul to break these walls,
To answer freedom when it calls.

At last parole, and skies so wide,
Yet fear ran deep, a rising tide.
But courage whispered, calm and clear,
"Zihuatanejo"—peace was near.

Beside the sea, where blue waves break,
I found the life I feared to take.
Now breathing air, forever free,
Redemption came, at last, for me.

Brooks Was Here

Inside the walls, he lived so long,
Where time was slow, yet life moved on.
A gentle man with weary hands,
Trapped behind the warden's plans.

His books were stacked, his duty clear,
To lend the words he held so dear.
Yet freedom came, and what was left?
A hollow shell, a heart bereft.

The world had changed, too fast, too loud,
The city streets, a nameless crowd.
No walls to guide, no bars to bind,
Just endless space—a caged-up mind.

He fed his bird, then tied the knot,
A fate the world had long forgot.
A simple note, carved deep and near:
"Brooks was here."

And in that phrase, so short, so grim,
He left a mark—they'd not leave him.

John Coffey's Light

A giant stood with weary eyes,
A gentle heart, so calm, so wise.
With shackled hands and head bowed low,
He bore a pain they'd never know.

The world had judged, yet knew him not,
A fate unfair, a crime he fought.
For in his hands, both rough and strong,
Lived healing power, pure and long.

He breathed in sorrow, pulled out pain,
Gave life away, yet none remained.
His gift a curse, too much to bear,
A burden worn with love and care.

"I'm tired, boss," he softly said,
Of hate and hurt, of fear and dread.
They flipped the switch—his soul took flight,
And left behind a world less bright.

The Gunslinger's Quest

Through barren lands and deserts wide,
A gunslinger rode with fate as guide.
His iron cold, his aim was true,
He walked the path that few men knew.

The tower called, a whispered dream,
A shadow cast in time's slow stream.
Through loss and pain, he forged ahead,
With ghosts behind and friends now dead.

Ka was cruel, yet he obeyed,
A broken heart, a hand well-played.
For though he fought with steady grace,
The wheel still turned—his endless chase.

Again he climbs, the same old track,
The horn now held—will he turn back?
Or is he bound to ride once more,
Through endless doors, through eldritch lore?

The world had moved, yet he remained,
Through riddles dark and battles strained.
A lonely knight with steel in hand,
Still chasing dreams on shifting sand.

He loved, he lost, yet carried on,
His path was bleak, his hope was gone.
Yet in his soul, a fire burned bright,
A whispered call, the Tower's light.

Was he the hero? Was he the foe?
The wheel still spins, yet none can know.
For Roland walks, and Roland tries,
And in the end, he never dies.

Annie Wilkes

In mountain snow, a house concealed,
Where twisted secrets lie revealed.
She nurses pain with smiles so sweet—
Beware the kindness you may meet.

A lonely writer trapped inside,
His shattered legs, his shattered pride.
Paul Sheldon lies in fear and dread,
Within the prison of her bed.

With eyes of madness, voice serene,
Annie Wilkes—a darkened queen.
Misery's keeper, fate's dark hand,
Her twisted love none understand.

Obsessed, possessed by tales she read,
In pages torn, her mind misled.
Her hammer swings, the pain so stark,
She breaks his bones, she leaves her mark.

Yet evil cloaked in gentle care,
Her brutal kindness hard to bear.
A nurse who heals and wounds the same,
Within her heart, a violent flame.

But courage fights through pain and gloom,
Escaping madness, escaping doom.
Annie's story ends in fright—
Her misery fades into night.

Firefly

Captain Tightpants

Through the black, the stars aglow,
A ship called *Serenity* dares to go.
With rusted hull and engines worn,
She flies defiant, free—reborn.

Her captain, rough yet strong of heart,
A soldier torn, a man apart.
Once he fought, and once he bled,
For a flag now lost, for the dead he led.

No chains shall bind, no law command,
He walks the 'Verse with gun in hand.
Not for wealth nor noble cause,
But for a crew that gives him pause.

Zoe's fierce, his war-time shield,
Loyal still, her word won't yield.
Wash's wit and River's mind,
Both too sharp for those behind.

Kaylee's hands keep engines bright,
Jayne just fights for coin and might.
Simon risks it all to stay,
Inara loves, but turns away.

Through Reaver tides and Alliance nets,
Through bounties placed and unpaid debts,
Malcolm stands, he will not kneel,
For freedom's more than just a deal.

So let them chase, let hounds be sent,
Let purple-bellies seek his scent.
They'll never break the man who flies,
Or take the fire from his skies.

Zoe, Warrior True

Through smoke and fire, steel and sand,
She fought beside a broken man.
With rifle raised and steady breath,
She stared unshaken into death.

Her soul was forged in battle's tide,
Where many ran, she stood with pride.
Though war was lost, she did not break,
She swore her oath for freedom's sake.

With Malcolm's word, she holds the line,
No fiercer friend you'll ever find.
Her loyalty's a bond unshaken,
By war, by pain, by fate forsaken.

Yet love still burns beneath her steel,
A warmth so deep, so strong, so real.
For Wash, she laughs, her light, her grace,
A softer soul in war's embrace.

She rides the Black where danger waits,
Defying men who tempt their fates.
No fear, no doubt, no backward glance,
A warrior's heart—she'll take the chance.

Through fire she walks, through storm she flies,
With battle's fury in her eyes.
A soldier, wife, and sister true—
A heart of steel, but love burns through.

Leaf on the Wind

A pilot born to touch the sky,
With steady hands and mischief's eye.
He danced through space with skill untamed,
And laughed at death, though none remained.

His wit was sharp, his spirit light,
A spark that burned against the night.
Through every chase, through every fight,
He steered *Serenity* just right.

With dinosaurs upon his dash,
He'd weave through wrecks and hardly crash.
A husband first, a warrior's love,
For Zoe, he was stars above.

He cracked a joke when fear ran high,
A smirk beneath the endless sky.
Yet when the war drums called him near,
He faced the dark without a fear.

A leaf upon the wind he soared,
Through danger's grasp, through cannon's roar.
And though his flight was cut too soon,
His name still shines beneath the moon.

The Heart of Serenity

With smudged-up hands and hopeful eyes,
She sees the world through sunny skies.
No engine cough, no worn-out gear,
Can dim the joy she holds so near.

She hums amid the grease and grime,
A tune as sweet as summer time.
Where others curse, she only grins,
And coaxes life from rust and spins.

Her touch can soothe, her skills amaze,
She keeps the ship through smoky days.
Where metal fails and circuits fry,
She works her magic, makes her fly.

A dress of frills, a blushing face,
A softer heart in darkest space.
She dreams of love, she dreams of light,
Yet never shuns the endless night.

Through all the trials, all the flight,
She is *Serenity's* delight.
For where there's Kaylee, there's a spark,
That keeps them flying through the dark.

The Doctor's Oath

He walked away from wealth and fame,
From fortune's light, from honored name.
A brother first, he chose to stand,
And risked it all with steady hand.

His voice is calm, his touch precise,
A healer's heart will pay the price.
Through fire and fear, through blood and bone,
He fights to keep his sister home.

A world of science left behind,
Yet still he heals, still he's kind.
Among the crew, a man apart,
Yet duty beats within his heart.

A cautious mind, a measured grace,
Yet love still finds a fleeting place.
For Kaylee's smile, so warm and bright,
Could pull him from the endless night.

No outlaw's heart, no soldier's blade,
But courage fierce and love that stayed.
A doctor's oath, a brother's will,
Through stars and war, defending still.

The Girl Who Sees

She whispers words that have no place,
Sees threads of time in endless space.
A dancer drifting through the dark,
A shattered mind, a burning spark.

They took her dreams, they stole her past,
And turned her thoughts to shadows cast.
Yet deep within, the fire remains,
A silent storm of joy and pain.

She moves like water, swift and free,
A leaf that bends but will not flee.
With deadly grace, with sharpened sight,
She wields the void, she owns the night.

Her brother's love, a tether strong,
A melody, a guiding song.
Through pain, through loss, through fear untold,
He held her hand, he would not fold.

Yet she's no ghost, no broken child,
Her spirit fierce, her heart is wild.
A warrior born, though none could see—
The girl who was, and still will be.

Grace Among the Stars

She moves with poise, with silken grace,
A quiet strength, a timeless face.
With every word, with every glance,
She bends the world as in a dance.

A woman born to gilded halls,
Yet chose the stars, their endless calls.
No chain, no law, no claim, no brand—
Her life her own, her heart unmanned.

She speaks with wit, with measured care,
A queen who rules the open air.
Yet love, unspoken, lingers near,
A wound she hides, a whispered fear.

For Mal, the rogue, the reckless fire,
Who sparks her heart, yet stirs her ire.
They stand apart, yet both belong,
A love unformed, a broken song.

She walks the black with knowing eyes,
A candle's glow 'neath endless skies.
Through war and loss, through love and pain,
She stays her course, she won't be tamed.

The Ballad of Jayne Cobb

A man of muscle, gun in hand,
He fights for coin, he takes his stand.
No noble cause, no grand ideal,
Just keep him paid, just cut the deal.

His words are blunt, his morals thin,
Yet when it counts, he just might win.
With Vera close and temper hot,
He shoots his way out of a spot.

He claims he ain't the hero kind,
Yet guilt can creep into his mind.
Regret once stirred his hardened chest—
The weight of lives he laid to rest.

For Jaynestown folk, he stands so tall,
A thief they loved despite it all.
Though he don't get the why or how,
A mudder's hymn still haunts him now.

He's rough, he's crude, he's oft unwise,
Yet in a fight, he earns his prize.
For when the chips fall, bullets fly,
You'll want Jayne Cobb to stand nearby.

The Preacher's Path

He walks the deck with steady grace,
A knowing look upon his face.
A shepherd's hand, a watchful eye,
Yet ghosts still linger when nights run high.

He speaks of faith, of wrong and right,
Of guiding souls through endless night.
Yet past the prayers and sacred lines,
A shadow waits, a past entwined.

A man of war? A man of peace?
The truth remains, but whispers cease.
For though he kneels, for though he prays,
His hands know well the soldier's ways.

No law he swears, no side he claims,
Yet mercy burns within his veins.
He stands, he speaks, he holds the line,
A voice of calm in darkened time.

And when the fire steals his breath,
He does not rage, he fears no death.
For what he knows, he cannot say,
But finds his peace and fades away.

Serenity's Song

She ain't no queen, she ain't no prize,
Just rust and steel 'neath open skies.
No regal halls, no polished grace,
Yet still she flies through endless space.

Her engines hum, her heartbeat strong,
A home for those who don't belong.
Through war and loss, through dark and dust,
She keeps them safe, she earns their trust.

Her hull is patched, her parts are worn,
Yet love has shaped the way she's borne.
For in her walls, through bolt and seam,
Lie hopes and hearts and broken dreams.

The law may chase, the black may call,
But she don't break, she don't fall.
A bird set free, a whispered name,
A soul of fire, a ship untamed.

So let them mock, let doubters sneer,
She'll find the stars, she'll persevere.
For home ain't walls, nor land, nor tide—
It's where you stand, it's where you ride.

M*A*S*H

Hawkeye Pierce: The Battlefield's Wit

In Korea's cold and war-torn land,
Where death and duty go hand in hand,
A surgeon worked with skill and grace,
And humor brightened up the place.

His name was Pierce—Hawkeye to all,
A doctor swift to heed the call.
With scalpel sharp and sharper tongue,
He saved the old, preserved the young.

Through blood-soaked nights and weary days,
He masked his pain in mocking ways.
A jester clad in olive green,
A soldier's heart forever keen.

He drank his gin, he cracked his jokes,
And took no joy in killing folks.
No love for war, no taste for strife,
He stitched the wounds, not took the life.

With Trapper gone and B.J. near,
He found new friends to share his cheer.
Yet loss still weighed upon his soul,
A toll that time could not control.

Through choppers' roar and mortar's blast,
He hoped each war would be the last.
But as the world ignored his cries,
He healed the broken, said goodbyes.

And when the war had reached its close,
He left behind the life he chose.
A hero not with sword or gun,
But hands that healed—his work was done.

B.J. Hunnicutt: A Heart Held True

Through war-torn nights and battle's din,
Where blood runs deep and lives wear thin,
A man stood firm with steady grace,
A gentle heart in a ruthless place.

His name was B.J., strong and kind,
A sharper wit, a sharper mind.
With hands that healed and eyes so bright,
He fought with skill, not guns, nor might.

No thirst for war, no taste for fame,
He played no part in glory's game.
Yet stitch by stitch and bone by bone,
He sent men safely back to home.

Through laughing jests and pranks so sly,
He helped the weary soldiers sigh.
A friend to all, a rock, a guide,
With Hawkeye ever by his side.

Yet far away, across the sea,
His wife and child called out to thee.
He longed for home with aching soul,
A missing piece, a heart not whole.

And when at last the war had passed,
He waved goodbye, went home at last.
But though he left, his work remained,
For love and loss had left him changed.

Henry Blake: A Leader's Farewell

In tents of green near battle's sound,
Where war and wounds were all around,
A leader stood with weary grace,
A kind heart in a ruthless place.

Henry Blake, both firm and fair,
A man who led with tender care.
With fishing tales and shirts askew,
He did his best—he muddled through.

Not one for rules or strict command,
Yet steady was his guiding hand.
He loved his crew, though times were tough,
And laughed when days grew dark enough.

Through Radar's words and Hawkeye's jest,
He took the madness, did his best.
A husband torn, a father too,
Who longed for home and skies so blue.

Then came the day he said goodbye,
A tear behind his smiling eye.
He left with hope, a dream in sight,
To hold his wife and kids that night.

But fate was cruel, the skies turned black,
His plane was hit—he won't come back.
The camp fell still, the laughter died,
As war stole one more life inside.

Though Henry's gone, his spirit stays,
In memories of brighter days.
A man of heart, both kind and brave,
Now rests beyond the waves.

Sherman Potter: The Soldier's Guide

With silver hair and steadfast grin,
Through war's cruel game so hard to win,
A leader stood, both firm and wise,
With steady hands and knowing eyes.

Sherman Potter, old yet spry,
A cavalry man in days gone by.
With tales of horses, dust, and ride,
He led with strength and love inside.

No nonsense, yet a heart so wide,
A guiding hand, a source of pride.
He ruled with care, not iron might,
And kept the camp from losing sight.

Through Hawkeye's pranks and B.J.'s fun,
He'd shake his head but let them run.
For through the jokes and hijinks wild,
He saw the hurt in every child.

With brandy poured and words well-spoke,
He soothed the pain where spirits broke.
A doctor first, a soldier last,
Who knew that wars must end—must pass.

And when the war had reached its close,
He left behind the life he chose.
To home he rode with heart set free,
To farm, to love, to memory.

Charles Emerson Winchester III: A Surgeon's Pride

In satin threads and tones refined,
A Boston man of learned mind,
With scalpel keen and standards high,
He met the war with shrewd reply.

Charles Winchester, proud and bold,
With manners stiff and heart untold.
He scoffed at jest, at crude display,
Yet found himself too far to stay.

Among the jokes and makeshift beds,
Where chaos reigned and hope had fled,
He fought against the grim design,
Demanding skill, precision fine.

A pompous air, a lofty stand,
Yet steady was his surgeon's hand.
No man of war, no brute nor knave,
He lived to heal, to mend, to save.

And though he sneered at jokes uncouth,
Beneath it stirred a deeper truth.
For when he found the war's own cost,
He learned the price of battles lost.

No final jest, no parting bow,
He left with more than he allowed.
For though he sought his world of grand,
He left a piece in that harsh land.

Margaret Houlihan: The Heart Beneath Steel

With spine of steel and voice so strong,
She kept the nurses right from wrong.
Through war's cruel tide and duty's call,
She gave her life—she gave her all.

Her name was Houlihan—so proud,
A woman fierce, a force unbowed.
With golden hair and fire inside,
She stood with strength, she walked with pride.

A soldier's child, she knew the game,
She lived for rank, she craved acclaim.
Yet through the mask of rigid grace,
A heart still beat beneath the face.

She loved too hard, she fought too fast,
She clung to love that couldn't last.
But when the truth came into sight,
She chose her strength, she chose her right.

Through wounds and loss, through blood and pain,
She held her own through war's cruel rain.
A leader strong, yet soft and kind,
A woman fierce, a heart refined.

And when the war had reached its close,
She left behind the life she chose.
No longer bound, no longer torn,
She walked away—her soul reborn.

Max Klinger: The Schemer with Heart

In silk and lace with heels so high,
A man would prance and plead and sigh.
Through war's dark haze and jungle heat,
He danced to dodge his army seat.

Max Klinger, wild, absurd, yet keen,
A Corporal dressed like a canteen queen.
With skirts that swayed and plans so grand,
He fought to flee this foreign land.

From wedding gowns to crimson frills,
He tried all tricks, defied all wills.
A Section Eight? His grandest dream—
Yet war outlasted every scheme.

But through the jokes and comic grace,
A deeper heart still held its place.
For when the wounded cried in pain,
He cast off games to help sustain.

A soldier's friend, a heart so wide,
He stood with strength, he stood with pride.
And though his fight for home was true,
He found a cause he never knew.

When war was done, he chose to stay,
Not bound by tricks or grand display.
For in that land so far, so torn,
Max Klinger found where he was born.

Radar O'Reilly: The Heart of the Camp

With ears so sharp and eyes so bright,
He sensed the choppers in the night.
Before the roar, before the sound,
He knew when wounded hit the ground.

Young and small, yet strong inside,
A boy who stood with soldier's pride.
From farm to war, from fields to tents,
He faced the world with innocence.

A teddy bear clutched in his grip,
Yet never once did duty slip.
With steady hands and knowing glance,
He kept the camp in perfect dance.

From papers signed to calls received,
He worked with faith—he still believed.
For in a place so filled with loss,
He found his way, he bore the cost.

But war is cruel, and youth must fade,
The light it dims, the heart it frays.
And when he saw the world had changed,
He knew it was his time to stray.

With tearful eyes and heavy soul,
He left behind the role he stole.
A boy no more, yet still so pure,
A heart of gold—his mark secure.

Father Mulcahy: A Shepherd in War

Through cries of pain and wounded calls,
Where bombs would shake the canvas walls,
A gentle voice, a steadfast guide,
Stood firm while war raged far and wide.

Father Mulcahy, kind and true,
A man of faith, a heart that knew,
That though the world was torn apart,
Hope still lived in every heart.

He blessed the lost, he held the weak,
He found the words when none could speak.
No gun in hand, no sword nor might,
Yet still he battled through the night.

A quiet strength, a soul so wide,
He knelt where men in anguish cried.
With prayers he fought, with love he led,
And gave them light through words he said.

Yet war would test his faith so deep,
Where death was real, and none could sleep.
But still he stood, his mission clear,
To heal, to serve, to calm the fear.

And when the war had reached its close,
He left behind the life he chose.
Yet in his steps, his voice remains,
A whisper soft through sorrow's pains.

Frank Burns: The Fool in Command

With rigid spine and jealous glare,
He stomped around with pomp and air.
A major fierce—at least in name,
Yet feared the fight, yet played the game.

Frank Burns, so strict, so full of pride,
But lacked the skill he wished to hide.
A surgeon slow, a leader weak,
Yet loud enough to sound unique.

With rules in hand and mind so small,
He sought respect but won none at all.
For while he'd sneer and throw a fit,
His hands would shake, his mind unfit.

With Margaret near, he felt so bold,
Yet love was weak, and hearts grew cold.
A sniveling man, so lost, so vain,
Yet trapped inside his own disdain.

Through Hawkeye's jokes and B.J.'s jabs,
He raged but fell with every grab.
For war would prove what men were worth,
And show the strength beyond one's birth.

Then came the day he left behind,
A man confused, a heart confined.
No cheers were sung, no tears were shed,
Just whispers soft: "He's gone," they said.

Goodbye, Farewell, and Amen

The war had raged, the years had passed,
But peace had found them all at last.
The sirens hushed, the guns grew still,
Yet hearts were torn, their souls were filled.

The camp was home through blood and strife,
Through loss and love, through death and life.
A place where laughter masked the pain,
Where jokes were shelter from the rain.

Hawkeye, weary, mind undone,
A doctor broken by the gun.
Yet in the end, he found his way,
To face the dawn of one last day.

B.J., strong, yet full of ache,
A friend to all, a bond to break.
He swore no words, no sad goodbyes,
Yet left his mark beneath the skies.

Potter stood with misted gaze,
A soldier's heart in autumn's phase.
He tipped his cap, he waved his hand,
And left for home, for peace, for land.

Klinger stayed, no dresses worn,
No need for schemes, no plans reborn.
For love had called, and fate had spun,
His war was fought, his race was run.

Father Mulcahy, calm and true,
Though war had robbed the sounds he knew.
Yet silence could not shake his grace,
His light still shone in time and place.

The choppers soared, the trucks rolled by,
The camp was gone, the fields ran dry.
Yet in the dirt, on earth so wide,
A final word was left with pride.

With stones arranged by B.J.'s hand,
A message carved across the land.
For Hawkeye saw, through tear-filled view—
One final word: a bold **GOODBYE**.

Almost Famous

In rock-and-roll's enchanted days,
A boy is swept into the haze.
Writing truths in lights and sound,
A music world that's lost and found.

William Miller, innocent eyes,
Dreams and truths he must comprise.
Young and hopeful, eager heart,
Music's magic from the start.

Penny Lane, mysterious, bright,
Golden glow in concert light.
"Band-Aid" girl, not groupie bound,
Secret pains beneath her crown.

Russell Hammond, guitar king,
Charisma bold, fame he brings.
Torn between success and art,
Conflict deep within his heart.

Jeff Bebe, singer proud,
Ego fragile, voice so loud.
Jealousy and tension rife,
Friendship tested, band's own strife.

Elaine Miller, worried, stern,
Mother's love, lessons learned.
Fearful yet supportive guide,
Trust and freedom must collide.

Anita Miller, sister bold,
Vinyl truths in records told.
Free-spirit heart, defiance strong,
Inspiring journey through each song.

Lester Bangs, wisdom clear,
Rock critic sage, advice sincere.
Truth he preaches, no pretends—
"Be honest, kid, don't make them friends."

Polexia, Sapphire, Estrella's crew,
Band-Aids loyal, spirits true.
Friendships bound in music's glow,
Life lessons deep they come to know.

Dennis Hope, business mind,
Manager slick, image refined.
Corporate greed, money's fame,
Authenticity lost in the game.

Dick Roswell, steady hand,
Manager first, friend second planned.
Balancing peace behind the scenes,
Chaos calmed by subtle means.

Ben Fong-Torres, Rolling Stone's face,
Deadline pressure, journal chase.
Editor firm, demands concise,
Truth in words, precise advice.

Vic Munoz, rival scribe,
Music world's competing vibe.
Challenges posed, pressures high,
Proving truth amid the lie.

In buses bound, across the land,
Stories born by Stillwater band.
Truth, illusion intertwined,
In search of meaning hard to find.

Love and heartbreak, fame's high cost,
Innocence gained and childhood lost.
Through friendship, lies, and truths revealed,
Life's painful growth cannot be sealed.

A coming-of-age beneath the stars,
Music's joy and hidden scars.
Almost famous, dreams pursued—
Lessons learned, forever viewed.

Shall We Play a Game?
A Poem Inspired by WarGames

A boy with a keyboard, a hacker with skill,
Searching for secrets, just chasing a thrill.
A system he finds with a challenge so bold,
A game filled with war, its dangers untold.

A missile screen blinks, the world on the line,
Numbers and targets, a countdown in time.
He thought it was harmless—just code on a screen,
But war isn't simple, and neither's the machine.

The sirens arise, the generals stare,
Fear in their eyes, a world unprepared.
Can logic and reason undo what's begun,
Before the last missile is fired and done?

The clock's racing forward, the codes locked in place,
The world at the edge of a nuclear embrace.
Yet lessons are learned when the system plays chess,
That no one can win in a game such as this.

The screen fades to black, the war fades away,
No battles were fought, no lives lost today.
But deep in the wires, the lesson remains
The smartest of minds must be wise with their games.

The Wolverines' Cry
A Poem Inspired by Red Dawn

The morning was quiet, the sky painted red,
Then shadows came falling, the whole town in dread.
Parachutes opened, like nightmares unfurled,
War had arrived in their small peaceful world.

A handful of friends with no time to grieve,
Fled to the mountains with plans up their sleeve.
Young hearts unbroken, though fear filled their veins,
They swore to fight back and break off the chains.

Through forests they crept, through rivers they ran,
Learning to strike with a soldier's demand.
With rifles in hand and revenge in their eyes,
They'd rather die free than surrender their lives.

The enemy hunted, but never could tame,
The spirit that burned in their blood like a flame.
For each one that fell, another would rise,
Wolverines roared 'neath the cold, bitter skies.

Through hardship and loss, through hunger and pain,
Their courage remained though the cost was insane.
And when the war ended, the echoes still called,
Of those who had fought, and those who had fallen.

The land may grow quiet, the years may move on,
But freedom once taken is never forgone.
For somewhere the mountains still whisper their name,
And Wolverines' courage still burns in the flame.

The West Wing

In corridors of power grand,
A President guides this land.
Ideals high and passions flow,
Decisions swift, solutions slow.

Josiah Bartlet, leader wise,
Integrity shines in his eyes.
Scholar's mind, compassion clear,
Steering nation through each year.

Leo McGarry, Chief of Staff,
Wisdom deep with steady laugh.
Loyal friend, strength defined,
Supportive heart, brilliant mind.

Josh Lyman, passion bright,
Political instinct sharp and tight.
Wit and charm, ambitious dreams,
Behind his smile, vision gleams.

C.J. Cregg, voice and grace,
Facing press with steady face.
Quick wit flows, honesty shown,
Courage clear, strength her own.

Toby Ziegler, thoughtful, stern,
Speechwriter whose phrases burn.
Idealist heart, words profound,
Justice sought, truths resound.

Sam Seaborn, bright and clear,
Optimist's hope forever near.
Speechcraft pure, vision bold,
Future's promise firmly told.

Donna Moss, loyal aid,
Smart and strong, ambition laid.
Learning quick, humor keen,
Growth displayed behind the scene.

Charlie Young, aide sincere,
Dignity calm, heart so clear.
President's trust, friendship deep,
Steady watch he always keeps.

Abbey Bartlet, First Lady bold,
Compassionate strength, courage untold.
Doctor's care and wisdom bright,
Partner true, guiding light.

Will Bailey, strategist new,
Words precise, purpose true.
Idealistic heart maintained,
Loyalty deeply ingrained.

Kate Harper, counsel wise,
Security clear, guarded eyes.
Advice firm, caution taught,
Danger faced, threats distraught.

Matt Santos, rising star,
Vision clear, dreams afar.
Integrity bold, ambition fair,
Hopeful change fills the air.

Arnold Vinick, rival bold,
Integrity clear, honesty told.
Statesman's heart, principles sound,
Respect between opponents found.

Margaret, Leo's voice sincere,
Efficient aide, wit severe.
Loyal heart, steady guide,
Humor dry, steadfast pride.

Ainsley Hayes, sharp and bright,
Legal mind, conservative sight.
Bridging gaps with charm and skill,
Unity sought, ideals fulfill.

Nancy McNally, voice secure,
Security strong, advice mature.
Protecting nation, steady hand,
Confidence bold, clear command.

In halls of power, dreams pursue,
Idealism tested, courage true.
Friendships firm, ambitions seen,
Hearts entwined behind the scene.

Bartlet's team, devoted cast,
Working hard from first to last.
Nation's hope, their endless quest,
Serving proudly, America's best.

The Americans

In shadows deep, behind disguise,
Spies live hidden, truth defies.
Secrets spun in silent homes,
Cold War battles quietly roam.

Philip Jennings, calm yet torn,
Loyalty strained, conscience worn.
Two worlds battled, heart and land,
Caught between duty and command.

Elizabeth Jennings, strong and cold,
Patriot fierce, beliefs controlled.
Mission bound, determined heart,
Love and duty worlds apart.

Stan Beeman, neighbor near,
FBI eyes, secrets clear.
Friendship tested, trust unsure,
Loyalty deep, intentions pure.

Paige Jennings, youthful eyes,
Truth uncovered, innocence dies.
Faith and family's strained embrace,
Finding purpose, finding place.

Henry Jennings, sheltered son,
Oblivious life, normalcy won.
Hidden truths behind his door,
Safe from dangers family bore.

Claudia, handler wise and stern,
Secrets taught, lessons learned.
Mother figure, ruthless care,
Nation first, compassion rare.

Gabriel, mentor, calm, refined,
Voice of reason, conscience kind.
Duty bound, yet human side,
Understanding, gentle guide.

Martha Hanson, trusting soul,
Innocent caught, losing control.
Love deceived by cunning lies,
Painful truths revealed through eyes.

Oleg Burov, Soviet son,
Idealist dreams, justice won.
Loyal heart yet conscience deep,
Risks he takes, secrets keep.

Nina Sergeevna, heart sincere,
Tragic journey, fate unclear.
Caught between two spying lands,
Bravery strong, hope withstands.

Frank Gaad, bureau chief,
Duty bound, hidden grief.
Integrity clear, courage known,
Leadership firm, trust is sown.

Dennis Aderholt, agent wise,
Careful watch, observant eyes.
Loyal partner, cautious friend,
Searching truths until the end.

Arkady Ivanovich, guidance clear,
Embassy voice, steady ear.
Diplomatic, cautious stance,
Balance sought through circumstance.

Mischa, Philip's distant son,
Searching father, journey begun.
Family secrets, fate defined,
Truths revealed, paths aligned.

William Crandall, scientist scared,
Deadly truths that he prepared.
Risked it all for greater good,
Conscience heavy, understood.

Through Cold War's chill, their lives unfold,
Secrets heavy, stories told.
Family, nation, truth, and lies,
Human hearts behind disguise.

In silent war, lives entwined,
Loyalty strained, hearts defined.
Spy or neighbor, friend or foe—
The cost of secrets none can know.

The Expanse

The Expanse

Beyond Earth's skies, in endless space,
A story starts, a frantic race.
Between the stars, the tensions rise—
Where humans dream and danger lies.

From asteroid belts to Martian lands,
The universe shifts in human hands.
James Holden leads a ragtag crew,
On Rocinante, brave and true.

Mars and Earth in fierce debate,
Belters fighting cruelest fate.
War drums pound, distrust is sown,
As alien seeds become full grown.

Protomolecule's chilling glow—
A force unleashed, mankind's great foe.
A gateway opens, worlds revealed,
And hidden truths no more concealed.

Yet heroes rise, their courage bright,
Amid the darkness, bringing light.
Through chaos, hope begins to dance,
Uniting hearts in wide expanse.

Across nine tales, worlds collide,
With stakes so high, no place to hide.
The human spirit tests its chance—
In Corey's epic, *The Expanse*.

James Holden

In space so vast, a lone ship flies—
The Rocinante, through dark skies.
James Holden leads, heart bold and clear,
A beacon bright, defying fear.

He stands for truth, though worlds oppose,
His honest heart creating foes.
From Earth to Mars, to Belt's rough crew,
Holden fights for what is true.

With loyal friends, his chosen kin,
He battles wars, again, again.
Naomi's love, his guiding star,
Together bound, through peace and war.

Protomolecule's deadly glow,
He faces threats no man should know.
Through gates unknown, he bravely goes,
Where darkness lurks and danger grows.

Idealist, stubborn, bold and free,
A symbol for humanity.
Holden sails through space's storm,
Hope and courage take their form.

Through chaos deep, he'll never bend,
A man whose faith will never end.
In darkest hour, he'll take his stance—
James Holden, heart of *The Expanse*.

Naomi Nagata

From Belt-born roots in shadows deep,
Where miners toil and secrets sleep,
Naomi rises strong and true—
An engineer, brave through and through.

With steady hands, she builds and mends,
Her skill unmatched, on her depends
The Rocinante's beating heart,
Her brilliance sets their ship apart.

Haunted by past decisions made,
Her courage firm, yet softly swayed,
Love and loss entwined as one,
She faces guilt, the damage done.

Beside James Holden, loyal, bold,
Her fierce resolve, a strength untold.
In chaos deep, she stands her ground,
A beacon when despair surrounds.

From Earth to Mars and gates unknown,
She fights for peace, her will has grown.
In darkest space, she holds the line,
Integrity her lasting sign.

Naomi Nagata, strong and bright,
A warrior heart, a guiding light,
In endless space, her spirit free—
The soul within *The Expanse's* sea.

Amos Burton

With eyes like steel and fists of stone,
A past he bears, but won't bemoan.
Amos Burton, rough and strong—
He walks a line of right and wrong.

In Baltimore's dark streets he grew,
Where mercy's thin, compassion few.
Yet through the pain, he learned to stand,
Survival etched upon his hand.

On Rocinante's fearless crew,
His loyalty fierce, his courage true.
Protector cold, yet deeply real,
He guards his own with forceful zeal.

No moral code, but friends to guide,
He trusts their hearts, walks by their side.
He battles foes with ruthless might,
Yet struggles hard to find what's right.

In darkest hours, his strength revealed,
A damaged soul behind his shield.
Though violence dwells within his core,
He fights for peace amidst the war.

Amos Burton, fierce and free,
A warrior's heart, complexity.
In chaos vast, he'll play his part—
The storm within *The Expanse's* heart.

Alex Kamal

A Martian born, with dreams of flight,
Alex Kamal, eyes sharp and bright.
At pilot's seat he feels at home—
Through endless stars, he's free to roam.

He guides the Roci swift and clean,
The smoothest hands space ever seen.
Through missile storms and battles fierce,
He steers his crew, and darkness pierce.

With Texas charm, his words are sweet,
His music plays, a steady beat.
Yet deep within, beneath his grin,
Lie doubts and fears he keeps within.

A loyal friend, he stands beside,
Protecting crew, his Martian pride.
In Holden's quest, he's always there—
Reliable, steadfast, and fair.

Though past mistakes weigh on his mind,
In space's cold he leaves behind
Regrets and guilt, to fight anew,
A better man, courageous, true.

Alex Kamal, through starry night,
A pilot brave, a guiding light.
Forever bound to chance and dance,
The steady hand of *The Expanse.*

Fred Johnson

Once known as "Butcher," stained by war,
A past of blood he can't ignore.
Fred Johnson wears the heavy weight
Of choices harsh, and bitter fate.

From Earth's proud fleet, his name disgraced,
To Belt he fled, his guilt embraced.
In shadows deep, he finds new cause,
A chance to heal, correct old flaws.

At Tycho Station, strong he stands,
Uniting Belters, forging plans.
Though trust is scarce and peace unsure,
Fred leads with strength and motives pure.

His voice a bridge, his goal is clear:
To break the chains of hate and fear.
A diplomat with warrior's heart,
He fights to mend what's torn apart.

Yet politics and war collide,
His enemies grow far and wide.
But Fred persists, his hope survives—
To build a world where freedom thrives.

Fred Johnson, seeking peace again,
A man reborn from loss and pain.
Once bound by war, now given chance—
Redeemed within *The Expanse*.

Chrisjen Avasarala

In silken robes with sharpest tongue,
Where power speaks, her words have stung.
Chrisjen rules with fierce command,
A queen who guides with steady hand.

Earth's mighty halls, her battlefield,
She sees through lies, the truth revealed.
With wit that cuts and words that burn,
Her foes respect, allies return.

Though harsh her voice, her heart is wise,
She bears the weight, makes sacrifice.
Behind bold eyes, compassion deep,
For Earth and Mars, for those who weep.

She fights for peace, yet battles fierce,
Through cunning moves, deception pierced.
In politics, her strength unmatched,
She shapes the peace from chaos hatched.

Yet family grounds her fierce intent,
Her love sincere, her spirit spent.
For humankind, she holds the line,
With iron will and mind divine.

Chrisjen, voice of Earth's advance,
A leader born of circumstance.
A fearless heart, prepared to dance—
The power behind *The Expanse*.

Bobbie Draper

Born beneath the Martian sky,
Her warrior's heart, her chin held high.
In armor strong, she faced the fray—
Bobbie Draper, bold and brave.

A soldier proud, her duty clear,
She fought for Mars without a fear.
Yet truths revealed would test her might—
Betrayed by those who hid the light.

From war to peace, she found her way,
Allies made in worlds astray.
Her courage firm, her purpose true,
A hero forged, her honor grew.

Beside Chrisjen, her faith restored,
In battles fierce, her spirit soared.
Protecting friends, her path defined,
A fighter strong, yet fair and kind.

With strength unmatched and loyal heart,
She faced the dark, she played her part.
A symbol bright of hope's advance,
A warrior's soul within *The Expanse*.

Breaking Bad

Breaking Bad

In desert dust and quiet night,
A teacher walks toward fading light.
A chemist skilled, his fate misled,
From timid man to king he fled.

Walter White, in illness bound,
A dying heart, a path he found.
Crystal pure, his empire rose,
Secrets hidden, no one knows.

Jesse Pinkman, troubled youth,
Caught in webs of bitter truth.
Cooking blue beneath the stars,
Guilt and sorrow leave deep scars.

Danger lurking, threat concealed,
Hank the lawman hot on heels.
Tension mounts with every scene,
Lives destroyed by blue and green.

Power gained but honor lost,
Every victory has its cost.
Greed and pride, a brutal test,
The devil whispered, "You're the best."

Empires built on shaky ground,
Blood and tears, a silence sound.
Heisenberg—a legend born,
Hat and glasses proudly worn.

But pride precedes a bitter fall,
Death and loss consume them all.
A tale of darkness, fierce and sad,
This breaking good turned breaking bad.

Walter White

In shadows cast by life's despair,
A gentle teacher, meek and fair,
Walter White, his fate unplanned,
A diagnosis forced his hand.

From chalk and class to darker days,
Chemistry changed in harmful ways;
Crystal pure, blue treasure made,
In hidden labs, his morals fade.

With Jesse, partner lost and found,
Cooking silent, underground.
Each batch refined, their fame would grow,
Secrets buried deep below.

Hat and glasses, cold disguise,
Heisenberg—his ruthless eyes.
Power, pride became his goal,
Trading piece by piece his soul.

Family torn by hidden sin,
Wealth and lies became his kin.
The monster rose from quiet man,
Consumed by greed and darker plan.

Yet empire built would soon collapse,
Caught by truth in bitter traps.
Fallen king, his reign undone,
Redemption lost, his race was run.

Walter White, both lost and grand,
A tragic tale in desert sand.
From humble start to bitter end,
Good intentions can't pretend.

Jesse Pinkman

In shadows dark, a troubled youth,
A heart of gold, yet lost to truth.
Jesse Pinkman, scarred and worn,
Lost in chaos, hopes forlorn.

With Walter White, he cooked the blue,
Secrets kept, and dangers grew.
From RV labs to distant plains,
Riches earned, yet bound in chains.

"Yo," he'd shout, a mask so tough,
Inside, though, he'd had enough.
Haunted by the deeds he'd done,
Dreams destroyed and friendships gone.

A loyal friend through dark and strife,
He sought escape, a better life.
But every turn brought more despair,
Sinking deeper, gasping air.

Torment followed Jesse's road,
Weighed down heavy, guilt his load.
Yet through pain, he found his might,
Fought the darkness, reached for light.

Surviving horrors none should see,
He broke the chains, at last set free.
Driving fast, he fled the past,
Freedom gained, relief at last.

Jesse Pinkman, scarred but bold,
Broken heart with strength untold.
A soul redeemed from paths gone bad—
A hero born from Breaking Bad.

Gus Fring

A quiet man, polite and neat,
Gus Fring smiles, calm and sweet.
A hidden king behind his mask,
Danger lurking in each task.

Owner of the chicken place,
Kind and gentle public face;
But secrets dark behind the scenes—
Power flows in silent streams.

Calculated, sharp, and cold,
Empire built on blue and gold.
Eyes behind those glasses hide
The ruthless plans he keeps inside.

In shadows deep, he plots with care,
Precision rules his icy stare.
Fear and calm, both intertwined,
His vengeance patient, well-defined.

But pride and power draw him near,
Blind him to the threats so clear.
His empire cracks, betrayal brews—
A chess game played, and soon he'll lose.

One final glance, a tidy tie,
Half in death, still dignified.
Gus Fring falls, his reign complete,
A gentleman brought to defeat.

Hank Schrader

Bold and brash, with hearty laugh,
Badge of honor marks his path.
Hank Schrader, tough and true,
Justice guides his every view.

DEA agent, strong and wise,
Hunting down each web of lies.
Tracking secrets, crimes untold,
Seeking truth, determined, bold.

Brother-in-law, friend sincere,
Trusting Walt without a fear.
Blinded by their family ties,
Never seeing Walter's lies.

Minerals gathered, beers in hand,
Moments peaceful, life so grand.
But beneath each laugh and joke,
Lurked a darkness that awoke.

When truth unraveled, painful, raw,
Betrayed by trust, betrayed by law.
Face to face with harshest fate,
Standing firm, defying hate.

In desert dust, with courage strong,
Staring down what's right and wrong.
Final words, defiant, brave,
He met his end—no man's slave.

Hank Schrader fell with noble heart,
Integrity his lasting art.
Badge of courage, honor clad,
Hero lost to Breaking Bad.

Friday Night Lights

Beneath the bright, warm Texas skies,
Where fields stretch wide, ambition flies,
In Dillon, football's sacred ground—
Where dreams are born and legends found.

Coach Taylor, wise and calm and strong,
With Tami near, where he belongs.
She counsels hearts and soothes the pain,
Their bond endures through sun and rain.

Clear eyes, full hearts, the team unites,
From Panther blue to Lions' fights.
Each Friday night, beneath those lights,
They chase their dreams, they climb new heights.

Jason Street, with fate unplanned,
Rises strong in life's tough hand.
Though paralyzed, his spirit grows—
His courage, strength, the whole town knows.

Tim Riggins, rugged, tough and wild,
Yet deep inside, a broken child.
Loyal friend, through ups and downs,
Heart of gold beneath his frowns.

Matt Saracen, quiet grace,
Bearing burdens, finding place.
Caring grandson, gentle soul,
Leads the team, fulfills his role.

Smash Williams, dreams so vast,
Running swift, outruns the past.
Through adversity he stands,
Victory shaped by his own hands.

Landry Clarke, with humor bright,
Best friend loyal, wrong or right.
Through awkward laughs, through moments tense,
Courage blooms and confidence.

Tyra Collette, tough and bold,
Breaking free from what she's told.
Rising high beyond life's chains,
Determined heart, she stakes her claim.

Lyla Garrity, poised yet torn,
Her path uncertain, love reborn.
Faith and doubt collide within,
Searching truth, a strength to win.

Vince Howard battles strife,
Seeking purpose, changing life.
From troubled youth to quarterback,
Finding hope, no looking back.

Luke Cafferty, farmer's son,
Hard work drives the battles won.
Heart sincere, with quiet fire,
Humble dreams, pure desire.

Becky Sproles, young and strong,
Facing hardships, finding song.
Her journey steep, yet bravely trod,
A fighter, growing against the odds.

Buddy Garrity, proud and loud,
Panther faithful, strong and proud.
Community's heart, through thick and thin,
Redemption found deep within.

In Dillon's glow, beneath the stars,
Stories told, revealing scars.
Lives intertwined, each tale unique,
In every loss, in every peak.

So when those Friday lights shine clear,
We see the heart, the dreams held dear.
Forever bonded, win or lose—
Clear eyes, full hearts, they cannot lose.

The Wire

In Baltimore's gray city streets,
Where good and evil daily meets,
A game is played, no rules defined—
A battle fought in hearts and minds.

McNulty seeks the hidden truth,
A stubborn cop, both bold and aloof.
His reckless ways, his fearless stare—
A hero flawed, beyond repair.

Bunk Moreland, wise with humor's charm,
Solves murders with a steady arm.
His laughter masks the weary toll,
Justice his ever-distant goal.

Kima Greggs, tough and smart,
With courage fierce and loyal heart.
Navigates the ruthless storm,
Where honor fights corruption's form.

Lester Freamon, quiet sage,
Patience deep beyond his age.
Through puzzles dark, his skill untold,
The clever mind, precise and bold.

Cedric Daniels, strong yet strained,
Balancing politics, justice maintained.
Leadership born from measured pace,
Integrity etched upon his face.

Avon Barksdale rules the block,
Kingpin standing firm as rock.
Street-wise sharpness, power vast,
Yet trapped by choices from his past.

Stringer Bell, a businessman,
In violence drawn, yet dreams a plan.
Ambitions soar beyond the street,
Where street and power fiercely meet.

Omar Little, legend feared,
A shotgun king, the streets revered.
A robber with a code, alone,
Injustice faced, revenge his own.

Bubbles fights addiction's chains,
Through desperate hope, enduring pain.
His heart is pure beneath despair,
A tortured soul, redemption rare.

Marlo Stanfield, cold as ice,
Controls the game at ruthless price.
In silence dark, ambition stark,
His empire built on hearts grown dark.

Michael Lee, young and strong,
Caught between what's right and wrong.
Forced to fight, protect his own,
In innocence lost, yet courage shown.

Bodie Broadus, loyal, brave,
Struggling from cradle to the grave.
Street-soldier's heart, eyes open wide,
Trapped in fate he can't outride.

Carver grows from reckless youth,
Learning slowly deeper truth.
Becoming leader, firm and fair,
Protecting those within his care.

Prez, whose flaws once brought disgrace,
Finds his purpose, second place.
Classroom hero, giving voice
To children bound by fate, not choice.

Prop Joe's wisdom, calm and smart,
Peacekeeper's role, a careful art.
Playing chess among fierce kings,
Trading words as power sings.

Snoop and Chris, cold-hearted pair,
Execute without a care.
Yet darkness hides behind their eyes,
Souls consumed by endless lies.

In Baltimore, the wire pulled tight,
Blurred lines between the wrong and right.
The city's heart exposed, laid bare,
Lives entwined in dark despair.

From cops to dealers, good and ill,
Each holds secrets, truths concealed.
A tale of struggle, hope, and pain,
The endless cycle starts again.

Through city streets, their stories told,
Forever marked, forever bold.
Truth and sorrow, hope and fire—
The human heart revealed by *The Wire*.

Lost

Upon an island strange and vast,
A plane goes down, the die is cast.
Survivors scattered, scared, alone,
Their hidden fates yet still unknown.

Jack Shephard leads, compelled to heal,
A troubled hero, brave and real.
Through chaos deep, he guides the lost,
His heart endures, despite the cost.

Kate Austen runs from past and pain,
Secrets guarded, guilt's dark stain.
Strong yet torn, her soul adrift,
She fights to heal, her burden lift.

Sawyer, rugged, brash and bold,
Cons and lies, his heart grown cold.
Yet beneath the tough disguise,
Lurks compassion in his eyes.

Locke believes in destiny's hand,
Faithful pilgrim in strange land.
Walking tall from chair once bound,
In mysteries deep his truths are found.

Hurley, kind with gentle soul,
Bearing luck he can't control.
Numbers haunt, his mind unclear,
Yet friendship brightens every fear.

Sayid, skilled yet scarred by war,
His heart is heavy, conscience sore.
Seeking peace, redemption's way,
A soldier's burden day by day.

Claire, sweet mother filled with love,
Guided by whispers from above.
Her child the hope she fights to keep,
Through visions dark and dreams so deep.

Charlie, rock star lost and found,
In music's grace and troubles bound.
Addiction's chains he tries to break,
His sacrifice for friendship's sake.

Sun and Jin, divided hearts,
Together bound, yet worlds apart.
Through struggles fierce their love remains,
Uniting souls despite their pains.

Michael searches, love his guide,
Father's quest with desperate stride.
For Walt he fights with every breath,
Facing shadows, fear, and death.

Walt, mysterious, gifted child,
Special powers, fate beguiled.
His disappearance, secrets deep,
Mysteries the island keeps.

Desmond Hume, through time displaced,
Love and hope forever chased.
Destiny's key, his visions clear,
Saving friends he holds so dear.

Ben Linus, cunning, cold, and sly,
Leader lost, yet reasons why.
His motives clouded, truth unclear,
His darkness hides his secret fear.

Juliet, gentle, fierce, and wise,
Hidden sorrow fills her eyes.
Her past concealed by quiet grace,
Her love sincere in silent place.

Boone and Shannon, siblings strained,
Together broken, bonds regained.
Tragedy marks their stories brief,
Yet leaves behind a lasting grief.

Mr. Eko, faith restored,
A man redeemed, peace explored.
His strength profound, his courage pure,
A soul reborn, his path secure.

Miles speaks to restless souls,
Their stories whispered, grief unfolds.
A skeptic voice with truth sincere,
Unlocking secrets buried here.

Faraday, scientist unsure,
Seeking truths obscure, secure.
Timelines twisted, knowledge vast,
His genius fights to change the past.

Charlotte searches island lore,
Secrets locked in earth's deep core.
Her memory fades, her purpose clear,
The island calls; her fate draws near.

Richard Alpert, ageless guide,
Eternal watcher, truths inside.
The island's voice, advisor's role,
His purpose bound to Jacob's soul.

Jacob weaves his endless thread,
Paths designed, the living led.
His rival, Man in Black, opposed,
In eternal struggle souls enclosed.

Upon this shore, the journey deep,
Their secrets bound, their wounds to keep.
Each character, a story crossed,
Together found, forever *Lost.*

OZ

Inside these walls of iron cold,
The tales of Oz are harshly told.
Emerald City, prison stark,
Where souls endure the endless dark.

Tim McManus dreams reform,
Idealist who braves the storm.
Seeking hope in deepest gloom,
Yet darkness fills each concrete room.

Warden Glynn, who holds command,
Keeps fragile peace by steady hand.
Balancing justice, law, and pain,
In Oz's world, a ruthless reign.

Tobias Beecher, lawyer turned,
In prison fires his soul is burned.
From broken man to vengeful heart,
Seeking peace, yet torn apart.

Chris Keller, charm and guile,
Seductive eyes, deceiving smile.
Danger wrapped in love's disguise,
His loyalty forever lies.

Vern Schillinger, ruthless hate,
Aryan leader seals his fate.
Cruelty masks his fearful soul,
Dominance his constant goal.

Simon Adebisi, fierce and wild,
Power hungry, anger's child.
Hat tilted low, eyes so cold,
His brutal tale forever bold.

Kareem Said, faith profound,
Muslim leader, voice resounds.
Struggles deep with pride and grace,
Seeking truth in darkest place.

Ryan O'Reily, cunning mind,
Manipulation redefined.
His schemes run deep, no trust to share,
Yet love for Cyril pure and rare.

Cyril O'Reily, childlike mind,
Innocent and lost in kind.
Dependent soul, protective love,
A fragile heart that's pushed and shoved.

Miguel Alvarez, proud yet torn,
Haunted by guilt, his spirit worn.
Seeking freedom, life defined,
Trapped within his troubled mind.

Augustus Hill narrates the tale,
Voice of reason behind the veil.
In wheelchair bound, wise and clear,
Truthful guide through hate and fear.

Leo Busmalis digs to flee,
Tunnel-dreaming endlessly.
Comic heart, though hope denied,
Persistence keeps his dream alive.

Bob Rebadow, gentle, wise,
Whispers truths with haunted eyes.
Elder statesman, calm in storm,
His visions cryptic, fate informs.

Father Mukada, priestly care,
Bearing burdens none would dare.
Confessions dark, sins revealed,
Healing wounds forever sealed.

Dr. Nathan, heart sincere,
Treating wounds both deep and clear.
Compassion fighting pain's despair,
Finding good in evil's lair.

Officer Murphy, steady guard,
Justice firm yet kindness hard.
Fairness guides his weary way,
Through violence faced day by day.

Clayton Hughes, conflicted heart,
Guard turned bitter, torn apart.
Consumed by hate, revenge and pride,
Loyalty lost, his soul denied.

In Emerald City, lives entwined,
Hope and fear forever bind.
Every inmate's secret crossed,
Humanity in darkness lost.

Within these walls, stories live,
Pain to take, love to give.
In OZ, the price forever high,
Where dreams are born, and dreams must die.

Stargate

Through ancient rings of stone and light,
A gateway opens, worlds in sight.
From Earth we step through starry doors,
Adventure bound on distant shores.

Jack O'Neill, the leader bold,
Sarcasm sharp, heart of gold.
A warrior's strength, a soldier's will,
Yet humor warms his courage still.

Daniel Jackson, scholar wise,
Searching truths with earnest eyes.
Languages ancient, meanings deep,
His passion strong, his friendships keep.

Samantha Carter, brilliant mind,
Science boundless, courage defined.
Invention sparks at her command,
A hero brave who takes a stand.

Teal'c, a warrior proud and true,
From Goa'uld chains he bravely flew.
Honor guides his loyal heart,
Strength and wisdom set apart.

General Hammond, steady guide,
Commanding voice with heart beside.
His courage calm, decisions clear,
Leader firm whom all revere.

Jonas Quinn, keen and bright,
Scholar learning truth and light.
In Daniel's absence, courage found,
His insights sharp, new paths unbound.

Vala Mal Doran, wild and free,
Trickster heart, complexity.
Yet loyalty beneath disguise,
Mischief sparkles in her eyes.

Cameron Mitchell, spirit bold,
New leader brave, in battles cold.
Uniting team with fearless heart,
Humor, strength, he plays his part.

Doctor Fraiser, healer kind,
Caring touch and brilliant mind.
Lives she saves with endless care,
Comfort found in trials unfair.

Thor, wise ally, noble friend,
Asgard wisdom, peace defends.
Alien guide through cosmic flight,
Honor shines through darkest night.

Jacob Carter, blended souls,
Tok'ra symbiote controls.
Father's love and wisdom clear,
Sacrifices calm yet dear.

Bra'tac, mentor, warrior wise,
Teaching strength with knowing eyes.
Jaffa's pride he does reclaim,
Courage burns within his flame.

Apophis, Goa'uld lord supreme,
His tyranny a ruthless dream.
Enemy fierce, his power vast,
Yet evil's reign will never last.

Ba'al, villain sleek and sly,
Manipulations, clever lies.
Charismatic, dangerous charm,
Spinning webs of hidden harm.

Atlantis calls through distant gate,
Sheppard leads to uncertain fate.
Rodney's mind with brilliance sparked,
Teyla's wisdom leaves a mark.

Ronon Dex, warrior strong,
Running from a past so wrong.
Brave companion, fierce yet true,
Atlantis team's protector new.

Elizabeth Weir, leader wise,
Diplomacy her greatest prize.
In troubled seas her voice so clear,
Courage calms the deepest fear.

Destiny journeys far from home,
Young commands through space unknown.
Rush, with brilliance, visions stark,
Searching truth within the dark.

Through stargate journeys, brave and bold,
Friendships forged and stories told.
From worlds unknown to Earth's own door,
Adventure calls forevermore.

Across the stars, their courage shown,
Hearts united, bonds full grown.
Exploring realms, their lives entwine,
Forever bound by gate divine.

NYPD Blue

In city streets, both dark and bright,
They guard the law, they fight the fight.
The Fifteenth Squad, a bond so true,
Cops tested hard in NYPD Blue.

Detective Sipowicz, gruff and worn,
A heart of gold beneath the scorn.
Battling demons, booze, and pain,
Yet courage flows within his veins.

John Kelly first at Sipowicz's side,
Steady, strong, a cop with pride.
His gentle strength, compassion clear,
A quiet hero, trusted, dear.

Bobby Simone, calm and wise,
With quiet strength behind his eyes.
Integrity guides every deed,
A noble man in word and creed.

Diane Russell, tough yet kind,
Battles scars within her mind.
Finding strength amid the storm,
Her courage deep, her heart reborn.

Greg Medavoy, quirky heart,
Nervous charm, yet does his part.
Awkward yet sincere, refined,
A gentle soul, compassion lined.

James Martinez, earnest, bright,
Seeks the truth, pursues what's right.
His youthful heart, loyalty strong,
Learning wisdom all along.

Jill Kirkendall, strength within,
Faces trials, truths begin.
Mother's care, detective's art,
Fierce protection fills her heart.

Danny Sorenson, troubled soul,
Restless heart, seeks control.
Wounds unseen, battles fierce,
Haunted eyes, where sadness peers.

John Clark Jr., young and brave,
Legacy his father gave.
Stepping boldly into place,
Determined spirit, earnest face.

Connie McDowell, tough yet fair,
Her burdens heavy, strength to bear.
Family love, protective will,
Justice guided by her skill.

Lieutenant Fancy, firm command,
Fairness guides his steady hand.
Balancing truth, loyalty clear,
Guiding all he holds so dear.

Lieutenant Rodriguez steps with pride,
Experience deep, leadership tried.
Cool under pressure, courage plain,
Leading the squad through stress and pain.

Rita Ortiz, fierce and strong,
Determined force, fighting wrong.
Yet softer side behind her shield,
Her warmth sincere, true heart revealed.

Baldwin Jones, calm yet tough,
His measured voice is strong enough.
Integrity guides every stride,
His wisdom deep, his conscience guide.

ADA Costas, justice's voice,
Balancing law with careful choice.
Her love for Sipowicz deep and clear,
Tragedy leaves scars severe.

PAA John, with humor dry,
Gentle kindness passing by.
Holding chaos calm in hand,
Steady voice within command.

In squad room tight, their bonds are made,
Trust and friendship, never fade.
Through crimes intense, emotions rise,
Humanity behind their eyes.

New York streets demand their best,
Each case resolved, another test.
The Fifteenth squad, forever true,
Hearts and courage, NYPD Blue.

The Golden Girls

In Miami sun, beneath bright skies,
Four golden friends share laughs and sighs.
Through cheesecake nights and stories told,
Life's never dull when friends grow old.

Dorothy Zbornak, tall and wise,
Sharp-tongued wit, sarcastic eyes.
Yet gentle heart and thoughtful mind,
Her warmth sincere, though words unkind.

Sophia Petrillo, mother bold,
Sicilian tales forever told.
Wisecracks sharp with endless sass,
Truth delivered bold as brass.

Rose Nylund, sweet and pure,
St. Olaf tales, surreal, obscure.
Naïve charm, innocent grace,
Heartfelt kindness lights her face.

Blanche Devereaux, Southern belle,
Romantic tales she'll gladly tell.
Confidence, charisma strong,
Passion bright her whole life long.

Stan Zbornak, Dorothy's pain,
Ex-husband back, again, again.
Salesman charm, yet bumbling grace,
Trouble wrapped in smiling face.

Miles Webber, Rose's beau,
Scholarly heart, steady and slow.
Patient soul, affection clear,
Love that holds through doubt and fear.

Sophia's wisdom, quick and sly,
No nonsense truths, she won't deny.
Though memory fades and age advanced,
Her strength in humor firmly danced.

Together bound through joys and tears,
Shared laughter echoing through years.
Friendships tested, bonds secure,
Through thick and thin, their love endures.

So gather round that kitchen light,
Where wisdom flows each sleepless night.
Four golden souls, forever bold—
True friendship's warmth will not grow old.

The X-Files

In shadows deep, where secrets lie,
Truth awaits beneath dark sky.
Two agents seek what's unexplained,
Facing truths and secrets chained.

Fox Mulder, driven, bold, sincere,
His quest relentless, path unclear.
Belief unshaken, mind unbent,
For sister lost, his life is spent.

Dana Scully, science bound,
Her rational voice firm and sound.
With skeptic mind yet loyal heart,
She seeks the truth, plays her part.

Skinner stands, authority clear,
Steady guidance, courage near.
Behind stern eyes, decisions weighed,
Loyalty deep, yet price is paid.

Cigarette Man, shadows cast,
Secrets hidden from his past.
Conspiracies spun, control refined,
Dark intentions intertwined.

Alex Krycek, traitor sly,
Betrayals swift, his loyalties fly.
Double dealings, shifting sides,
Truth concealed by endless lies.

Deep Throat whispers cryptic clues,
Trust uncertain, truth diffused.
Informant brave, his warnings stark,
Guiding path through dangers dark.

Mr. X, with guarded face,
Secrets given, hidden grace.
Fearless eyes, warnings cold,
His courage bold, his purpose old.

The Lone Gunmen, trio wise,
Truth in darkness, no disguise.
Langly, Frohike, Byers stand,
Hackers brave, truth their brand.

Monica Reyes, spiritual guide,
Believing truths the heart can't hide.
Insight deep, intuition clear,
Facing mysteries others fear.

John Doggett, tough and brave,
Integrity guides every wave.
Searching justice, hardened heart,
Truth pursued with earnest start.

Marita Covarrubias, hidden ties,
Diplomat with watchful eyes.
Loyalty masked, her motives veiled,
Alliances carefully detailed.

William, child of fate unclear,
Prophecies surround his fear.
Mulder, Scully's precious son,
Destiny entwined, begun.

From alien tales to cryptic lore,
FBI files hold secrets more.
The truth remains just out of reach,
A promise sought yet hard to breach.

Together bound by trust and quest,
Agents face each secret test.
The truth is out there, hearts align,
Forever searching X-Files sign.

Cold Case

In Philly streets, old secrets sleep,
Where justice waits in silence deep.
Forgotten crimes, unanswered pain—
Until the truth can breathe again.

Lilly Rush, detective true,
Bringing closure overdue.
Compassion guides her steady heart,
Unraveling mysteries, worlds apart.

Scotty Valens, strong and clear,
Protective soul, emotions near.
Past wounds haunt his guarded eyes,
Yet courage fights beneath disguise.

Lieutenant Stillman, wise and calm,
Guiding hands and steady palm.
Father figure, trusted guide,
Justice bound with quiet pride.

Nick Vera, gruff yet kind,
Humor masks the pain inside.
Streetwise heart, relentless pace,
Loyalty marked upon his face.

Will Jeffries, veteran proud,
Memories strong, voice aloud.
His steady wisdom, stories told,
History clear, experience bold.

Kat Miller, fierce yet fair,
Mother's love, detective's care.
Balance strong between her roles,
Truth pursued, no hidden goals.

Josie Sutton, brief but bright,
Bold and fearless in the fight.
Short-lived stay, but strength sincere,
Her passion lasting, crystal clear.

ADA Kite, justice's voice,
Seeking truth, careful choice.
Lilly's heart once touched his own,
Love and justice briefly known.

Frannie Ching, kind and smart,
Gentle strength, a warm, soft heart.
Forensic skills that truths reveal,
Careful eyes and insights real.

Louie Amante, cautious friend,
Questions deep and trust to lend.
By Scotty's side through troubled days,
Loyalty clear in subtle ways.

Each case reopened, victims heard,
Justice served by every word.
Voices silenced now awake,
Stories freed, for truth's own sake.

Philadelphia's past unearthed,
Secrets solved, renewed rebirth.
Each life reclaimed, no longer lost—
Cold case warmth, at any cost.

The Shield

In Farmington, beneath dark skies,
Justice blurred by twisted lies.
Where heroes fall, corruption breeds,
And guilty hearts disguise their deeds.

Vic Mackey leads, tough and bold,
Badge of honor cheaply sold.
Morals bent, yet family true,
His loyalty fierce, though lines askew.

Shane Vendrell, reckless friend,
Impulsive moves, morals bend.
Conflicted soul, regret concealed,
Betrayal deep, fate soon revealed.

Curtis Lemansky, heart sincere,
Loyalty strong, conscience clear.
Haunted eyes, tormented mind,
In chaos caught, compassion blind.

Ronnie Gardocki, quiet strength,
Cautious moves at careful length.
Silent partner, shadows deep,
Secrets held he's forced to keep.

Claudette Wyms, justice pure,
Voice of reason, firm and sure.
Steady hand through storm and strain,
Integrity guides through loss and pain.

Dutch Wagenbach, sharp and smart,
Solving crimes, his truest art.
Awkward charm, intellect bright,
Seeking truth through darkest night.

David Aceveda, driven pride,
Politics mixed, ambition tied.
Balancing power, secrets spun,
Goals pursued, battles won.

Julien Lowe, faith and doubt,
Personal truths, secrets shout.
Struggling hard to find his way,
Identity fought day by day.

Danny Sofer, strength within,
Duty calls, life begins.
Mother's courage, cop's resolve,
Life's tough puzzles she must solve.

Tina Hanlon, learning fast,
Mistakes made but quickly passed.
Innocence fades, wisdom grows,
Streetwise heart slowly shows.

Steve Billings, cynic, sly,
Sarcastic wit, lazy eye.
Yet hidden skill behind disdain,
Unseen talents still remain.

Monica Rawling, brave reform,
Challenging corruption's storm.
Bold and firm, her vision clear,
Change pursued, though short-lived here.

Antwon Mitchell, streetwise king,
Ganglord ruthless, violence brings.
Charismatic, dark control,
Power absolute, fierce and cold.

Kavanaugh hunts corrupt deeds,
Obsessive heart, justice breeds.
Crossing lines, vendetta deep,
Truth exposed, revenge to reap.

Corrine Mackey, torn and tried,
Vic's betrayals multiplied.
Mother brave, protecting sons,
In shadows deep, her courage runs.

Farmington's heart beats wild and tense,
Corruption hidden by pretense.
In darkest deeds, no truths concealed,
Justice blurred behind the Shield.

Game of Thrones

In Westeros, beneath dark skies,
A deadly game, where honor dies.
Seven kingdoms, blood and fire,
Kings and queens with fierce desire.

Ned Stark, lord of honor's call,
Truthful heart, destined to fall.
Winter's voice, courageous, bold,
Yet secrets deep his fate controlled.

Jon Snow, bastard, brave and true,
At the Wall, his courage grew.
Facing threats beyond the night,
Finding honor in the fight.

Daenerys Targaryen, Mother, queen,
Dragon's blood, a soul serene.
Breaker of chains, fire reborn,
Her destiny both praised and scorned.

Tyrion Lannister, sharp and wise,
Small in height, great in size.
Wit unmatched, his tongue of steel,
He plays the game, his wounds conceal.

Cersei Lannister, proud, refined,
Ambition dark, control defined.
Power's taste her endless quest,
A ruthless queen, fierce unrest.

Jaime Lannister, golden knight,
Honor stained, yet seeks the right.
Conflicted heart, complex desire,
Redeeming flame through trial and fire.

Arya Stark, fierce and strong,
Warrior trained, vengeance long.
Changing face, deadly skill,
Justice served with iron will.

Sansa Stark, innocence lost,
Survival found at brutal cost.
Strength concealed behind calm eyes,
Queenly poise, wisdom wise.

Bran Stark, visions clear,
Three-eyed Raven drawing near.
Destiny bound to ancient tree,
Secrets hold his prophecy.

Robb Stark, young wolf king,
Battles fought, fate's cruel sting.
Bravery bound by betrayal's knife,
Love and honor cost his life.

Theon Greyjoy, pride and shame,
Identity lost, seeks reclaim.
Broken spirit, tortured soul,
Redemption found in final goal.

Samwell Tarly, heart sincere,
Courage found within his fear.
Scholar brave, friend so true,
Knowledge deep, his valor grew.

Jorah Mormont, knight exiled,
Daenerys loved, devotion styled.
Protector fierce, loyalty deep,
Love unspoken, secrets keep.

Davos Seaworth, honest man,
Smuggler turned to noble plan.
Advisor wise, integrity clear,
Loyalty bound to kings sincere.

Melisandre, priestess red,
Magic flames, visions fed.
Faith and fire, prophecies told,
Secrets dark, truths unfold.

Brienne of Tarth, honor bright,
Knightly heart, courage's sight.
Oathkeeper firm, sword in hand,
Integrity's shield across the land.

Sandor Clegane, the Hound's dark way,
Violence masks the deep dismay.
Hidden heart beneath harsh face,
Redemption sought through quiet grace.

Littlefinger spins his webs,
Mastermind whose promise ebbs.
Chaos ruled, ambition high,
Schemes unfold until goodbye.

Varys, Spider whispering near,
Secrets held, intentions clear.
For the realm, his purpose stands,
Shaping fate with careful hands.

Stannis Baratheon, justice stern,
Throne he seeks, yet lessons learned.
Rigid heart, ambition burned,
Destiny harsh, cruelly turned.

Ramsay Bolton, evil's face,
Sadistic lord, devoid of grace.
Cruelty unmatched, soul undone,
Justice found beneath cold sun.

Euron Greyjoy sails to rule,
Pirate king, ambition cruel.
Madness shines in ruthless eyes,
Chaos follows, virtue dies.

Through fire, ice, and trials deep,
Promises made, hard to keep.
Westeros, a throne's dark claim,
A deadly dance—a Game of Thrones.

The Walking Dead

A world consumed by endless dread,
The living hide from walking dead.
Survival fierce, a struggle grim,
Humanity's hope grows frail and dim.

Rick Grimes, sheriff brave and true,
Leads survivors old and new.
Through loss and pain, courage deep,
A promise made, his group to keep.

Daryl Dixon, tough and cold,
Tracker fierce, yet heart of gold.
Silent strength, loyal friend,
Protector fierce until the end.

Carol Peletier, meek no more,
Survival taught her heart to roar.
Mother's pain transformed to might,
Fearless soul in endless fight.

Michonne, warrior sharp and wise,
Katana swift, defiant eyes.
Haunted past, yet hope restored,
Strength and grace within her sword.

Glenn Rhee, quick and bold,
Resourceful heart, courage told.
Love sincere for Maggie clear,
Bravery strong, facing fear.

Maggie Greene, farmer's child,
Strong and fierce, yet warm and mild.
Leader's heart, survivor's grace,
Resilient spirit guides her place.

Carl Grimes, child of strife,
Youthful heart transformed by life.
Lessons learned through painful years,
Courage conquers deepest fears.

Negan smiles with deadly charm,
Lucille swings with ruthless harm.
Villain's heart, charisma deep,
Darkness hidden, secrets keep.

Hershel Greene, wisdom clear,
Father figure, loved and dear.
Hopeful eyes, belief held fast,
Guiding voice through storms that passed.

Andrea, fighter brave and free,
Justice bound by tragedy.
Lost between what's wrong and right,
Her journey ends in sacrifice.

Shane Walsh, friend turned foe,
Jealous heart, emotions flow.
Loyalty fades to deadly rage,
Friendship shattered, lost on stage.

Tyreese, strength and gentle heart,
Peaceful man forced to fight's art.
Compassion clear, honor's call,
Standing firm until his fall.

Sasha, fierce yet scarred inside,
Battles grief she cannot hide.
Courage strong, defiant stance,
Choosing freedom, final chance.

Eugene Porter, mind precise,
Cowardice his great device.
Through fear he learns bravery's claim,
Redemption earned, a lasting name.

Abraham Ford, soldier tough,
Fighting hard, life's bitter rough.
Heart of gold behind the force,
Duty guides his fearless course.

Father Gabriel, faith unsure,
Coward turned courageous pure.
Finding strength through trials deep,
Redemption earned, promises keep.

The Governor rules by fear and lies,
Tyrant cold, humanity dies.
Power sought at darkest cost,
His soul consumed, forever lost.

Morgan Jones, peace and strife,
Haunted man reclaiming life.
Balance found between two sides,
Justice served, truth abides.

Rosita Espinosa, bold and strong,
Warrior fierce, righting wrong.
Survivor's heart, steady aim,
Resilient soul, earned acclaim.

Judith Grimes, born to strife,
Symbol bright of future life.
Innocence preserved with care,
Hope restored in darkest air.

Together bound by loss and dread,
Facing fears, defeating dead.
Love and courage fiercely bred—
Alive within the Walking Dead.

Jeremiah

In a world destroyed, adults no more,
Children left to face what's in store.
Civilization's shattered ground,
Hope and courage newly found.

Jeremiah leads with vision clear,
Searching truths beyond the fear.
Haunted by his father's quest,
Bravery guides him through the test.

Kurdy Malloy, strong and true,
Friendship forged, a bond that grew.
Fighter fierce, yet wise and kind,
His heart as strong as ties that bind.

Markus Alexander, leader wise,
Thunder Mountain's hope, disguise.
Building peace from broken lands,
Future shaped by steady hands.

Mister Smith, with visions deep,
Prophet burdened, secrets keep.
Truth revealed in cryptic dreams,
Faith restored, not as it seems.

Erin, fierce, a warrior's heart,
Strong resolve right from the start.
Bravery shines, loyalty bright,
Her courage steady in the fight.

Lee Chen, guard with loyal eyes,
Duty firm, yet trust he buys.
Integrity marks every deed,
Silent strength fulfills each need.

Theo, leader, wisdom sharp,
Freedom found beneath a tarp.
Her courage clear, conviction bold,
Truth and honor firmly hold.

Libby, kindness gentle, pure,
Healer's heart and love secure.
Hope restored through care sincere,
Compassion calms the deepest fear.

Elizabeth, strategist's mind,
Plans devised, solutions find.
Strength within her cautious glance,
Building peace through circumstance.

Sims, dark villain's ruthless hand,
Tyrant ruling troubled land.
Cruelty marked in every deed,
Power fed by endless greed.

Brothers of the apocalypse near,
Secrets dark, their presence clear.
Threatening peace, sowing pain,
Battles fought through storms and rain.

Together bound, survivors fight,
Seeking dawn beyond the night.
In darkness deep, their courage clear,
Faith renewed, hope draws near.

In Jeremiah's quest to find,
Truth and peace for humankind.
Friendships forged in troubled land,
Together strong, together stand.

Babylon 5

In deepest space, where races meet,
A station stands, its heart complete.
Diplomacy's uncertain art,
Where peace begins or wars can start.

Jeffrey Sinclair, commander brave,
Destined truths he longs to save.
Valen's mystery, ancient past,
His fate entwined, his shadow cast.

John Sheridan, captain bold,
Rebellion's voice, a heart of gold.
Z'ha'dum faced with fearless eyes,
Courage fierce, he defies lies.

Delenn, ambassador wise, serene,
Minbari grace and strength unseen.
Hybrid soul, a bridge defined,
Unity's hope for all mankind.

Michael Garibaldi, vigilant, tough,
Security chief, loyal enough.
Battling demons deep within,
Integrity strong, yet temptations begin.

Susan Ivanova, strength and wit,
Sarcasm sharp, with fire lit.
Heart concealed behind firm face,
Pain and love, courage and grace.

Londo Mollari, proud, complex,
Ambition strong, his soul perplexed.
Centauri pride, a tragic fate,
Redemption lost, but found too late.

G'Kar, warrior, prophet clear,
Narn resistance, without fear.
Transformed by pain to wisdom deep,
Hope and peace he longs to keep.

Stephen Franklin, healer's touch,
Compassion strong, caring much.
Healing wounds both seen and deep,
Battling shadows others keep.

Vir Cotto, gentle, pure,
Innocent heart, courage sure.
Voice of reason, quiet stand,
Strength concealed by trembling hand.

Marcus Cole, ranger bold,
Noble fighter, stories told.
Sacrifice pure, love concealed,
Hero's heart by fate revealed.

Lennier, loyal aide, sincere,
Faithful, wise, yet burdened clear.
Duty strong, yet love denies,
Painful truths behind calm eyes.

Lyta Alexander, psychic guide,
Telepathic powers, vast inside.
Vorlon touched, mysterious art,
Secrets deep within her heart.

Alfred Bester, Psi Corps cold,
Mind-control his power bold.
Villain sleek with hidden pain,
Justice twisted, cruel refrain.

Talia Winters, mind concealed,
Truthful heart, yet fate unsealed.
Betrayed by Corps, her trust misled,
Secrets deep within her head.

Zack Allan, loyal, steady guard,
Integrity firm, though choices hard.
Trust and duty intertwined,
Bravery marked, courage defined.

Kosh, Vorlon cryptic, wise,
Truth obscured by hidden eyes.
Mysteries spoken, silence deep,
Secrets ancient that he keeps.

Babylon 5, where stars align,
Heroes fight and fates combine.
In darkest night, their courage bright,
Uniting hope to win the fight.

A thousand voices, stories spun,
War and peace, lost and won.
Legacies born in distant skies,
Forever marked by Babylon 5.

Silicon Valley

In valley bright where tech dreams rise,
Ambitions soar, hope fills the skies.
Startups bloom, ideas ignite,
Success or failure overnight.

Richard Hendricks, shy and bright,
Genius coder, awkward plight.
Pied Piper's dream, compression's art,
Innovation born from heart.

Erlich Bachman, loud, absurd,
Confidence in every word.
Incubator's king, obscene,
Investor dreams, schemes unseen.

Gilfoyle, dark with biting wit,
System admin, skillful grit.
Cynical, yet loyalty clear,
In code he trusts, in humans fear.

Dinesh Chugtai, sharp and vain,
Coding skills with endless strain.
Competitive, friendship's twist,
Sarcastic charm, hard to resist.

Jared Dunn, sincere and kind,
Company first, heart aligned.
Nervous yet deeply wise inside,
Loyalty steadfast, gentle guide.

Monica Hall, steady friend,
Guiding dreams from start to end.
Honest heart in VC's lair,
Advice sincere, her judgments fair.

Gavin Belson, ego vast,
Hooli king, control steadfast.
Ambitions high, ruthless scheme,
Vision blurred by prideful dream.

Big Head, luck and fortune's child,
Oblivious, success compiled.
Talent vague, his wealth absurd,
Fame and fortune undeserved.

Laurie Bream, robotic cold,
Logic clear, emotions sold.
Raviga queen, precise and stark,
Decisions swift, analytical mark.

Russ Hanneman, billionaire wild,
Tres Commas king, ambition styled.
Extravagance, chaos unchained,
Disrupting lives, his ego untamed.

Nelson Bighetti, father's stress,
Stumbles into great success.
Innocence matched with comic fame,
Accidental wins his claim.

Jack Barker, salesman's flair,
Leadership style beyond compare.
Aggression bold, vision skewed,
Corporate dreams misunderstood.

Jian-Yang, sly and cruel,
Pranking schemes, a roommate duel.
Broken English, cunning smile,
Business plans built on guile.

Ron LaFlamme, lawyer slick,
Negotiations swift and quick.
Protecting assets, bending rules,
Playing smart among the fools.

Hoover, Gavin's loyal guide,
Assistant trapped, dignity tried.
Quiet strength beneath the pain,
Endless patience under strain.

In tech's bright lights, their fate entwined,
Success and failure, closely aligned.
Friendship tested, rivalries spun,
The endless chase to be number one.

Dreams compressed, and fortunes made,
Silicon Valley's endless parade.
Through laughter, pain, they all persist—
Innovation's comic twist.

24

Ticking clock, each second clear,
A nation's fate hangs ever near.
Terror's shadow dark and deep,
Secrets that Jack Bauer keeps.

Jack Bauer, fearless heart,
Agent fierce, playing part.
Sacrifice, his life's true test,
Fighting terror, never rest.

Tony Almeida, trusted friend,
Loyalty strong until the end.
Betrayal faced, heart still true,
Redemption found in actions new.

Nina Myers, sly and cold,
Agent turned, betrayal bold.
Secrets hidden, deadly lies,
Trust destroyed, forever ties.

David Palmer, noble, wise,
President with truthful eyes.
Integrity guides through the fight,
Justice firm, defending right.

Kim Bauer, troubled child,
Danger follows, life beguiled.
Strength discovered, lessons learned,
Courage found as trust returned.

Chloe O'Brian, tech and wit,
Hacking genius, humor lit.
Friendship loyal, skills profound,
Guiding Jack through dangerous ground.

Michelle Dessler, brave and smart,
Courage firm, devoted heart.
Leader strong, choices bold,
Love and duty closely hold.

Bill Buchanan, calm, sincere,
Leadership steadfast and clear.
Voice of reason, guiding hand,
Justice served at his command.

Curtis Manning, brave and bright,
Agent strong in every fight.
Steady heart, moral guide,
Duty bound until he died.

Audrey Raines, diplomat fair,
Love and duty, painful care.
Bound to Jack by love and strife,
Tragedy shapes her tortured life.

Charles Logan, power's greed,
Weakness hidden, darkened seed.
President flawed, lies unfold,
Secrets kept, betrayal bold.

Renee Walker, fierce and bold,
Agent brave, her story told.
Morals tested, lines she crossed,
Truth pursued at bitter cost.

Morris O'Brian, charm and skill,
Humor masks a haunted will.
Struggles deep, yet courage found,
Love and duty, closely bound.

Edgar Stiles, loyal, sincere,
Tech expert, heart so clear.
Sacrifice made, ending brave,
Life laid down, friends to save.

Wayne Palmer, brother strong,
Legacy proud, righting wrong.
Courage tested, leadership tried,
Duty calls, no place to hide.

Aaron Pierce, steadfast guard,
Integrity firm, honor hard.
Protector true, president's shield,
Bravery bright, never yield.

Dina Araz, mother torn,
Loyalty strained, conscience worn.
Family bound by deadly fate,
Choices made, but far too late.

Mike Novick, counsel wise,
Politics his sharp disguise.
Advisor's voice, both strong and calm,
Navigating fear and harm.

Day by day, hour by hour,
Threats arise, betrayals sour.
Lives entwined in danger's core,
Twenty-four hours, nothing more.

Jack's resolve, unmatched, sincere,
Fighting threats both far and near.
Sacrifices deep, unspoken pain,
Guarding freedom, time again.

Through ticking clocks and endless strife,
Each choice defines a nation's life.
In darkest hours, hope remains,
The strength that Jack Bauer sustains.

Mr. Nobody

In choices made, in paths untried,
Life splits apart, worlds collide.
Each road taken, branches grow,
Futures many, none can know.

Nemo Nobody, life's enigma,
Bound to choice's endless stigma.
Every decision made or missed,
Creates new worlds that coexist.

Anna, love profound and pure,
Childhood friend, attraction sure.
Soulmate bound by fate's deep ties,
Love enduring, no disguise.

Elise, passion burning bright,
Fiery heart, chaotic light.
Tormented soul, deep despair,
Painful love beyond repair.

Jean, steady, calm, serene,
Perfect life, predictable scene.
Quiet sadness, hidden ache,
Safe and steady, love's mistake.

Father, kind yet burdened deep,
Loss and sorrow secrets keep.
Guiding hand, compassionate heart,
Father's love, worlds apart.

Mother, distant, cold withdrawn,
Heart detached, affection gone.
Choices made, forever split,
Family fractured, truth admit.

Young Nemo, eyes wide, sincere,
Facing choice, consumed by fear.
Innocence weighed by heavy chance,
Youthful heart in life's harsh dance.

Old Nemo, memories vast,
Infinite lives, present, past.
Wisdom deep, reflections flow,
Truth of choice, he seeks to know.

Journalist, searching clear,
Answers sought, future near.
Interviewing mysteries deep,
Secrets locked, the truth he'll keep.

Dr. Feldheim, science voice,
Fate and chance within his choice.
Theories deep, life's unknown,
Paths revealed, yet truth unshown.

Through shifting timelines, stories blend,
Lives beginning, lives that end.
Infinite ways, fate designed,
Realities twisting, intertwined.

In Nemo's heart, the answers hide,
Life's true meaning, deep inside.
No choice wrong, no path denied—
All truths live on, none subside.

Mr. Nobody, endless tale,
Existence vast, beyond the veil.
Infinite love, infinite pain,
Life's true mystery will remain.

Terra Nova

In future bleak, Earth fades away,
A distant world calls them to stay.
Through time's deep portal, hope restored,
A colony brave, new lands explored.

Jim Shannon, father brave and strong,
Protects his family, righting wrong.
Courage boundless, heart sincere,
Facing dangers without fear.

Elisabeth Shannon, healer wise,
Doctor skilled with caring eyes.
Family bound by love and grace,
Finding strength in this new place.

Josh Shannon, teenage pride,
Rebellion tempered deep inside.
Loyalty tested, lessons learned,
Bravery earned as trust returned.

Maddy Shannon, curious mind,
Science girl, adventures find.
Wisdom bright, intelligence clear,
Seeking knowledge far and near.

Zoe Shannon, youngest light,
Child's wonder, joy so bright.
Innocence pure, heart of gold,
Hopeful spirit, brave and bold.

Commander Taylor, leader bold,
Secrets guarded, strength untold.
Tough but fair, his mission clear,
Protecting those who gather here.

Skye Tate, friend yet mystery deep,
Secrets dark her soul must keep.
Torn between two worlds apart,
Trust and truth divide her heart.

Mira leads the Sixers fierce,
Loyal heart, intentions pierced.
Conflict deep with Taylor's reign,
Motives mixed, trust hard to gain.

Lucas Taylor, genius flawed,
Father's rival, fate outlawed.
Mind consumed by past and pain,
Betrayal marks his troubled name.

Lieutenant Washington, courage clear,
Second-in-command sincere.
Duty bound, honor's call,
Steadfast friend, loyal to all.

Mark Reynolds, soldier brave,
Maddy's love, devotion gave.
Courage shown in danger's face,
Protector firm, honor's grace.

Malcolm Wallace, scientist keen,
Knowledge vast, motives unseen.
Friend or rival, trust unsure,
Secrets deep his heart obscure.

Boylan, tavern owner sly,
Deals and whispers passing by.
Neutral heart, profit's game,
Secrets traded without shame.

Curran, troubled soldier scarred,
Mistakes made, redemption hard.
Loyalty tested, courage found,
Second chance on fertile ground.

Dinosaurs roam, threats abound,
New world dangers quickly found.
Survival fierce, family ties,
Together strong, hope never dies.

In Terra Nova, past made new,
Second chances shining through.
Family bonds forever stand,
Courage bound on ancient land.

Back to the Future

In Hill Valley, quiet town,
Adventure waits when time breaks down.
A young man's life is set to spin,
Past and future intertwined within.

Marty McFly, guitar dreams,
Life disrupted, time's extremes.
Courage bold, yet trouble-bound,
Time-travel secrets he has found.

Doc Emmett Brown, genius wild,
Science bright, imagination styled.
Flux Capacitor, brilliance pure,
Time's inventor, dreams secure.

George McFly, timid soul,
Fearful heart, lacks control.
Stories locked within his mind,
Courage deep he soon must find.

Lorraine Baines, youthful grace,
Romance bound by time's embrace.
Future mother, passion true,
Destiny shaped by moments new.

Biff Tannen, bully bold,
Ruthless power, heart so cold.
Future dark if unchecked fate,
Time's correction can't come late.

Jennifer Parker, loyal, sweet,
Marty's love, sincere and neat.
Future promised, yet unclear,
Trusting heart, devotion near.

Principal Strickland, tough and stern,
Discipline strict, lessons learned.
Guiding youth, authority clear,
Rules upheld, no slackers here.

Einstein, faithful canine friend,
Time's first traveler, no pretend.
Trusted sidekick, loyal heart,
Testing science, crucial part.

Clara Clayton, Doc's romance,
Love across time's great expanse.
Gentle soul, adventurous heart,
Destined bond, a fresh new start.

Griff Tannen, future threat,
Chaotic force, no regret.
Aggression wild, impulsive rage,
Danger bound in future's stage.

Old Biff Tannen, cunning, sly,
Twisting fate, his schemes imply.
Greedy heart, dark intent,
Altering timelines, chaos sent.

Seamus McFly, ancestor wise,
Guiding voice, gentle eyes.
Family values, courage deep,
Legacy strong, truths to keep.

Time machine, DeLorean bright,
Stainless steel through day and night.
88, speed attained,
Flashing sparks, futures gained.

Hoverboard flights, daring chase,
1955's frantic race.
Lightning strikes, clock tower's height,
Fate restored within the night.

Mistakes corrected, past restored,
Futures bright, new paths explored.
Lessons learned, courage displayed,
Love endures, no longer swayed.

In Hill Valley, destiny spun,
Time's great journey now is done.
Friendship bound, adventure's end,
Back to the Future—time to mend.

Billy Joel

From Long Island shores he came,
Piano keys would spark his fame.
Melodies both sweet and bold,
Telling stories often told.

In early days, he chased a dream,
Songs that flowed just like a stream.
"Cold Spring Harbor," humble start,
Honest voice, a hopeful heart.

"Piano Man," his timeless song,
Crowds would cheer and sing along.
Scenes of life in bars portrayed,
Classic tune that never fades.

"The Stranger" came, his rise begun,
"Just the Way You Are," hearts won.
"Movin' Out" with steady drive,
Scenes of dreams and hopes alive.

"52nd Street" brought soulful beats,
Big Shot tales from city streets.
Honesty, a tender tone,
Jazz-infused, a style his own.

"Glass Houses," energy high,
"Still Rock and Roll," youthful cry.
Attitude with rocker's flair,
Bold and brash, a daring air.

Songs of innocence and heart,
"Uptown Girl," fresh new start.
"An Innocent Man," tribute sound,
Vintage charm, acclaim renowned.

Social conscience, truth displayed,
"Allentown," hard times portrayed.
"Goodnight Saigon," friends who fell,
War and loss he sang so well.

"Storm Front," late-eighties flair,
"We Didn't Start the Fire," dare.
History rapid, passion strong,
Memories stirred within the song.

"River of Dreams," spiritual flight,
Searching souls through sleepless night.
Questions deep in rhythmic flow,
Final album long ago.

Madison Square, sold-out nights,
Piano keys beneath bright lights.
Crowds in awe, applause and cheer,
His music timeless, crystal clear.

Honors earned and legacy,
Storyteller, honesty.
Words and melodies refined,
Voice of generations lined.

Billy Joel, his music true,
Decades pass, yet always new.
Through ups and downs, he plays it all,
Piano man who answered call.

Expeditionary Force

When alien war engulfed the Earth,
Human courage found new worth.
One young soldier, far from home,
Across the stars was forced to roam.

Joe Bishop, brave and clever lead,
Calm and resourceful in each deed.
With wit and guts, he faced the fight,
Keeping hope through darkest night.

Skippy the Magnificent, unmatched AI,
Beer-can shaped, sarcastic guy.
Ego vast, intelligence grand,
Solving crises, always planned.

Emily Perkins, scientist bright,
Cool-headed logic, steady light.
Courage hidden, wisdom keen,
Trusted mind behind the scene.

Margaret Adams, captain bold,
Leadership clear, command controlled.
Steadfast heart, authority strong,
Guiding crew through battles long.

Lieutenant Smythe, dry and wry,
British charm, humor sly.
Sarcasm sharp, loyalty deep,
Friendship strong, trust to keep.

Chang, skilled pilot, fearless ace,
Maneuvering through danger's space.
Steady hands and nerves of steel,
Mastering flight with calm appeal.

Lieutenant Reed, warrior true,
Courage clear, devotion through.
Braving fights with strength refined,
Tactical force, battle defined.

Major Simms, steady force,
Trust and friendship set the course.
Mission first, yet heart displayed,
Solid ground in chaos frayed.

General Nagatha, leader stern,
Military tactics learned.
Decisions tough, weight severe,
Duty-bound, courage clear.

Chotek, Kristang ally found,
Warrior past, new trust profound.
Redemption sought through loyalty's strain,
Alliance built from former pain.

Ruhar, allies once unknown,
Hamster-like race, friendship grown.
Enemies turned to trusted friends,
Peace achieved where war suspends.

Elder races, hidden scheme,
Pulling strings behind the scene.
Secrets dark and mysteries vast,
Ancient truths revealed at last.

Together, this unlikely crew,
Facing dangers ever new.
Skippy's brilliance, Bishop's heart,
Humor sharp, a perfect art.

Through galaxies they boldly roam,
Protecting Earth, defending home.
Adventure deep, friendship strong,
Expeditionary Force moves on.

The Martian

Mars, the red and distant ground,
Where silence rules, no earthly sound.
A man left stranded, fate unplanned,
Survival bound to barren land.

Mark Watney, brave and smart,
Scientist, humor's art.
Resourceful heart, inventive mind,
Hope sustained, solutions find.

Melissa Lewis, captain fair,
Leader calm with steady care.
Courage strong, decisions made,
Guilt and duty firmly weighed.

Rick Martinez, pilot keen,
Humor bright in space unseen.
Trusted friend, steady guide,
Flying skill and endless pride.

Beth Johanssen, tech profound,
Systems managed, calm unbound.
Gentle heart, wisdom clear,
Quiet strength, facing fear.

Chris Beck, doctor wise,
Healing touch and steady eyes.
Courage firm, compassion deep,
Life protected, trust to keep.

Alex Vogel, scientist bold,
Logic calm, emotions hold.
Precision guides his steady hand,
Team united by command.

Vincent Kapoor, NASA face,
Steady voice with measured pace.
Seeking ways to bring Mark home,
Never resting, courage shown.

Teddy Sanders, cautious lead,
NASA head, tough choices heed.
Risk averse, yet mission clear,
Balancing hope against fear.

Mitch Henderson, bold and true,
Flight director, courage through.
Risking rules for what is right,
Standing firm in hardest fight.

Annie Montrose, press refined,
Sharp-tongued voice, truths aligned.
Facing public, brave and strong,
Speaking clear when plans go wrong.

Bruce Ng, the JPL mind,
Solutions clever, quick designed.
Innovation's brilliance bright,
Helping Watney's desperate fight.

Rich Purnell, genius shy,
Orbit plan, hopes rely.
Eccentric heart, vision deep,
Saving Watney, plans to keep.

Mindy Park, observant eyes,
Tracking Mars beneath vast skies.
Discovering life's subtle clue,
Hope restored, rescue due.

Together bound across vast space,
Uniting hearts in rescue's chase.
Determined minds, courage bright,
Returning hope through darkest night.

Mars' silent ground, now filled with cheer,
Human spirit conquers fear.
Watney's smile, victory's sign—
Science, courage intertwined.

www.ingramcontent.com/pod-product-compliance
Lightning Source LLC
Chambersburg PA
CBHW051921240626
47153CB00004B/1311